Vanessa the Choreography Fairy

For Bethany Ann and Megan Rose Middleton-Hunt,
with lots of love

Special thanks to Sue Mongredien

ISBN 978-0-545-48476-3

Previously published as *Pop Star Fairies #3: Vanessa the Dance Steps Fairy* by Orchard U.K. in 2012.

12 11 10 9 8 7 6 5 4 3 2 13 14 15 16 17 18/0

Printed in the U.S.A. 40

This edition first printing, March 2013

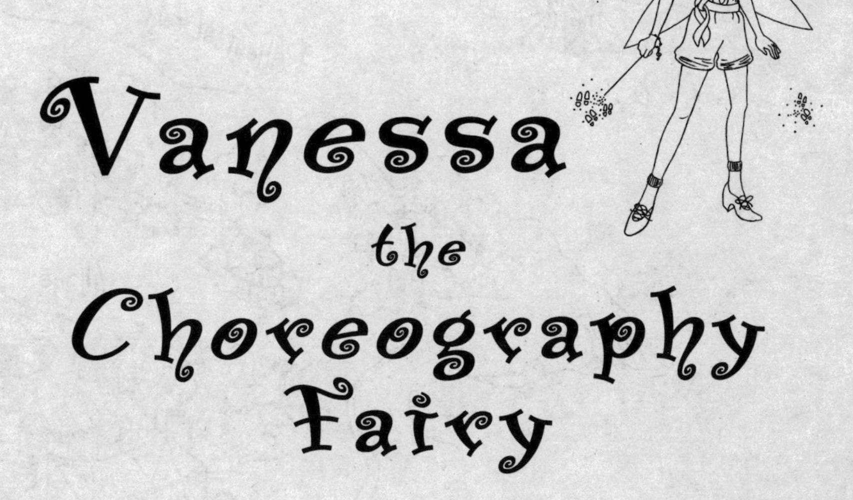

Vanessa the Choreography Fairy

by Daisy Meadows

SCHOLASTIC INC.

Fairyland Music Festival
A-OK trailer
Rehearsal tent
Star Village
Picnic hill
Beach

Jack Frost's Ice Castle
Campsite
Girls' tent
Main Stage
Karaoke tent
The Harbor
Café
Rainspell Island

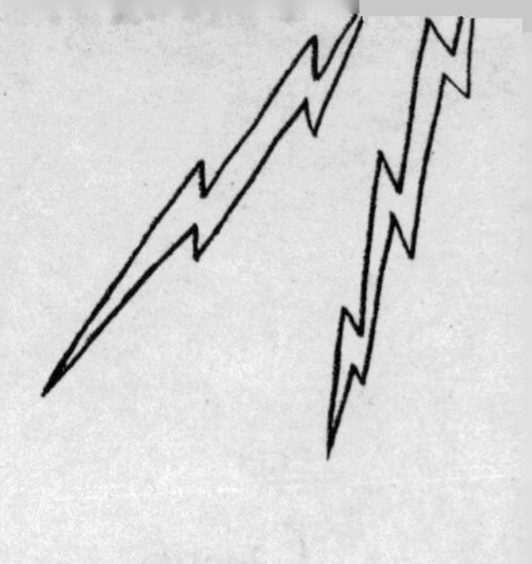

It's about time for the world to see
The legend I was born to be.
The prince of pop, a dazzling star,
My fans will flock from near and far.

But superstar fame is hard to get
Unless I help myself, I bet.
I need a plan, a cunning trick
To make my stage act super-slick.

Seven magic clefs I'll steal –
They'll give me true superstar appeal.
I'll sing and dance, I'll dazzle and shine,
And superstar glory will be mine!

Festival Fun 1

A Dance Disaster 11

Here Come the Boys! 25

Kirsty Has a Plan! 35

Dance-off Drama 47

Stage Magic 59

"Hooray!" cheered Rachel Walker, as she and her best friend, Kirsty Tate, walked along Rainspell Beach. "The sun is shining, we're on vacation together, *and* we're at the Rainspell Island Music Festival."

"It's been wonderful so far, hasn't it?" Kirsty agreed with a smile.

It was certainly turning out to be a day the girls would never forget. First, they'd seen their favorite band, The Angels, open the show. Next was the boy band A-OK, who'd wowed the crowd with their melodic harmonies. And best of all, Kirsty and Rachel had found themselves caught up in an exciting new fairy adventure, this time with the Superstar Fairies!

"Hi, girls," chorused three familiar voices.

Rachel and Kirsty turned to see Lexy, Serena, and Emilia — also known as The Angels.

“Hi,” said Kirsty. She and Rachel had met the band a while ago, when they’d helped Destiny the Rock Star Fairy. Now they were friends. The girls in the band had even given them backstage passes to the festival! Being friends with pop stars was almost as much fun as being friends with the fairies!

“Did you see A-OK? Weren’t they fabulous?” said Lexy.

“I didn’t know they were such great performers,” said Emilia, kicking off her sandals and wiggling her bare toes in the golden sand. “Those boys rocked!”

"I can't wait to see Sasha Sharp tonight," Rachel added. "She's such a good dancer."

"Sasha's amazing," Serena agreed. "Have you seen the video for her new song, 'Let's Dance'? She does such a cool routine. How does it go again?"

The Angels started singing Sasha's latest hit, and they all tried to remember the dance moves.

"Up, down, spin around, and touch
the ground,
Come on, everybody! Let's dance
around town.
With a hop to the left and a jump
to the right,
Come on, everybody! Let's dance tonight."

It was hard dancing on the sand, though. It wasn't long before Kirsty and

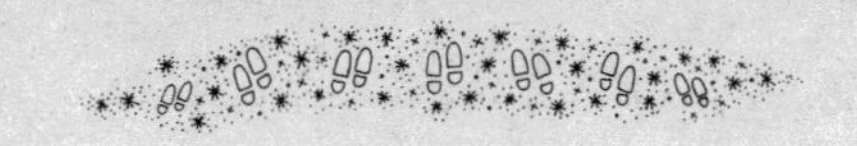

Rachel bumped into each other and
fell over.

"Whoops!" Kirsty giggled, brushing
sand off her clothes. "I think we need
some practice, Rachel."

"Well, there's a dance class starting soon in Star Village if you want to join," Serena told them. Star Village was a group of tents at the festival site where you could try all kinds of superstar activities — dance, fashion design, makeup, and singing lessons.

Lexy winked. "I heard there's going to be a special surprise there, actually," she added mysteriously.

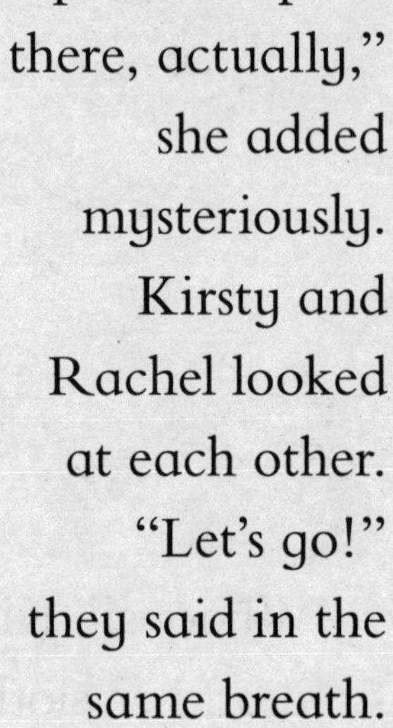

Kirsty and Rachel looked at each other.

"Let's go!" they said in the same breath.

The two friends said good-bye to The Angels and hurried toward the dance tent. It was late in the afternoon now, and the sun was sinking in the sky. The festival was as busy as ever, with lots of stalls selling clothes and jewelry, and the delicious smells of hot dogs and burgers wafting from food trucks.

"I wonder what the surprise will be," Rachel said. "We've already had so many other exciting surprises today, I can't imagine what else could possibly happen."

Rachel was right — the girls had enjoyed one surprise after another since they'd come to Rainspell Island that morning! First, they'd been whisked off to Fairyland by Destiny, who'd invited them to watch the rehearsals for the Fairyland Music Festival. It was wonderful to be back in Fairyland, but unfortunately, the rehearsals hadn't gone as planned. Mean Jack Frost had stolen the Superstar Fairies' seven magic clefs. The clefs helped make sure that superstars everywhere performed well. Without their clefs, even the Superstar Fairies struggled with high notes, tricky dance moves, and a lot more!

Jack Frost wanted to become a superstar himself, and had taken the magic clefs to the Rainspell Island Music Festival so that he could use their powers. So far, the girls had helped Jessie the Lyrics Fairy and Adele the Voice Fairy get their clefs back from the goblins, who were watching them for Jack Frost! But five clefs were still missing. If Kirsty and Rachel couldn't find them in time, the festival might be ruined.

"This has definitely been one of the most exciting days of my life," Kirsty said as they reached Star Village. "I can't wait to see what happens next!"

A Dance Disaster

Rachel and Kirsty found the big dance tent right away and went inside.

"Hi there," said a friendly lady wearing a purple leotard and leggings. She had corkscrew curls held back by a headband with a swirly pattern. "I'm Tamara, Sasha Sharp's assistant. Welcome to our dance class."

"Hi," Rachel said. "Do we need to wear special clothes for the class?" she asked, noticing that lots of kids had arrived in leotards and dance skirts. Some of them were sitting on the floor, trying on dance shoes.

"No," Tamara said, "but you can borrow some dance shoes if you want. Help yourselves." She led them to a rack full of shoes in all colors and sizes. Kirsty chose a lilac pair, and Rachel found some bright pink ones. There were small shoe mirrors placed around the tent so that the kids could see how they looked.

The girls went to a quiet corner and took off their sandals. Kirsty was just about to slip her foot into her dance shoe when there was a bright flash of color. To her surprise, a little fairy fluttered out in a shower of rainbow-colored fairy dust! "Oh!" Kirsty gasped. "Hello there."

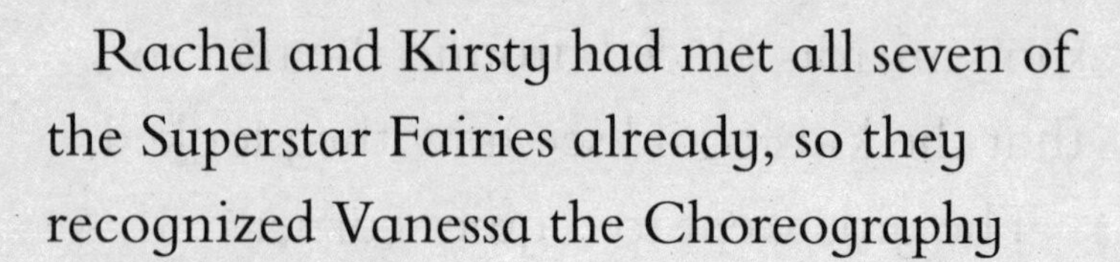

Rachel and Kirsty had met all seven of the Superstar Fairies already, so they recognized Vanessa the Choreography Fairy because of her lilac-colored felt hat. She was also wearing a short blue jumpsuit with halter straps. Her pink lace-up dance shoes had a chunky heel.

"Hello," Rachel said excitedly. "How are you? Have you found your magic clef yet?"

Vanessa shook her head. "No," she said. "And look what's been happening without it!"

She waved her wand at one of the small shoe mirrors. There was a flurry of sparkles, and then a scene appeared. The girls recognized the Fairyland Music Festival stage, then saw the Dance Fairies walk on to begin their rehearsal. Kirsty and Rachel knew what talented dancers the Dance Fairies were — but not today! The scene in the mirror showed them crashing into one another, tripping, and dancing out of sync.

"Oh, no," Rachel said, wincing as Serena the Salsa Fairy fell off the stage.

"They're even worse than we were on the beach," Kirsty said, remembering how they'd fallen over.

Vanessa gave a big sigh. "I'm worried about Sasha Sharp's performance," she said. "If I don't get my magic clef back in time, she'll be dancing badly, too — and so will everyone else at the festival."

Before the girls had a chance to reply, they heard Tamara's voice. "OK, everyone, our special class is about to begin," she announced. "Could you please form two rows in front of the stage? This way!"

Kirsty looked around to see a raised stage at the far end of the tent. But where was Tamara, exactly? "I guess we should go," she said.

"Vanessa, why don't you hide in my pocket?" Rachel suggested, pulling it open so that the little fairy could flutter inside. "We'll keep an eye out for your clef."

Rachel and Kirsty lined up with the other kids, even though there was still no sign of the dance teacher. Then the lights dimmed, and clouds of purple smoke poured from the side of the stage. A single spotlight appeared, revealing the shadowy shape of a dancer wearing a leotard and high heels.

Music blasted from the speakers, and Kirsty recognized the catchy opening to "Let's Dance." A huge cheer filled the tent.

"Up, down, spin around, and touch the ground . . ." went the song, and on the word *up*, the dancer on stage leaped high into the air. Unfortunately, she landed awkwardly and tumbled right off the stage, falling at Kirsty's and Rachel's feet with a *thump*!

"Oh my gosh, are you all right?" Rachel gasped, bending down to help her up.

At that moment, the music stopped and the lights came on again. As the tent was flooded with light, the girls realized that the dancer was none other than Sasha Sharp herself! They couldn't believe it!

The room filled with gasps as the other kids recognized her, too. Sasha gave a shaky laugh and got up, with Rachel and Kirsty both helping her. "Thanks, guys," she said. Then she smiled sheepishly at

the audience. "That was a lesson in how *not* to start your dance routine . . . especially since I'm hoping some of you will join me on stage tonight, as my backup dancers!"

There was stunned silence for a second — and then the tent erupted with excitement. Some girls yelled and hugged one another. Others, like Rachel and Kirsty, jumped up and down and cheered. This must be the surprise The Angels had been talking about!

"You're serious? You're really going to let some of us up on stage for your concert?" Kirsty asked Sasha in delight. The festival kept getting better and better!

Sasha grinned. "Oh, yes," she said. "Cool surprise, huh?"

"The best!" Rachel laughed. She hoped that she and Kirsty would be picked to dance!

"OK," Sasha said, climbing back on stage. "So let's practice. Copy me and we'll see how things go. Are we ready? One, two, three . . . hit it!"

The opening notes of "Let's Dance" sounded through the tent once more, and everyone copied Sasha's starting position. Rachel and Kirsty watched carefully as the famous star led them through the routine. It wasn't too complicated, but however hard they tried, everyone kept making mistakes. Not even Sasha could keep up with the footwork!

"I don't know what's wrong with me today," she grumbled as she lost her balance for the third time. "I've danced this routine so many times I thought I could do it in my sleep."

Rachel heard Vanessa sigh from where she was still tucked in her pocket. "It's because my magic clef is missing," the fairy murmured. "We have to get it back, otherwise Sasha and her dancers are going to be in all kinds of trouble tonight!"

Here Come the Boys!

"Let's take one more try," Sasha said wearily. "From the top!"

The rehearsal began again, but it quickly turned into chaos once more. Some dancers jumped up when they should have been crouching down, while others slid sideways when they should have been spinning around. Just as the whole thing was starting to look hopeless, four boys arrived late to the class and joined in. They were wearing bright green leotards and big, feathery hats that covered their faces.

"They're good," Kirsty whispered, noticing their graceful movements.

The boys *were* good, Rachel thought, stopping to watch — much better than anyone else there. They leaped high on the word *up*, landed perfectly on the word *down*, then gracefully spun around and touched the ground each time.

As the song finished, the rest of the crowd clapped for the boys, and so did Sasha. "Hey! You guys did that perfectly," she cheered. "Way better than I've been dancing, that's for sure." She leaned down and rubbed her ankle, wincing. Clearly it was still hurting from when she'd fallen on it before.

Tamara had noticed that Sasha was in pain, and joined her on the stage. "OK, everyone, now it's up to you to practice," she called out. "Let's meet back here at six o'clock for a final rehearsal."

The kids began filing out of the tent, still humming the song and chatting excitedly about the show that evening. Kirsty and Rachel put their sandals back on as Sasha limped to the side of the stage. Meanwhile, Tamara was briskly gathering all the star's belongings. With various

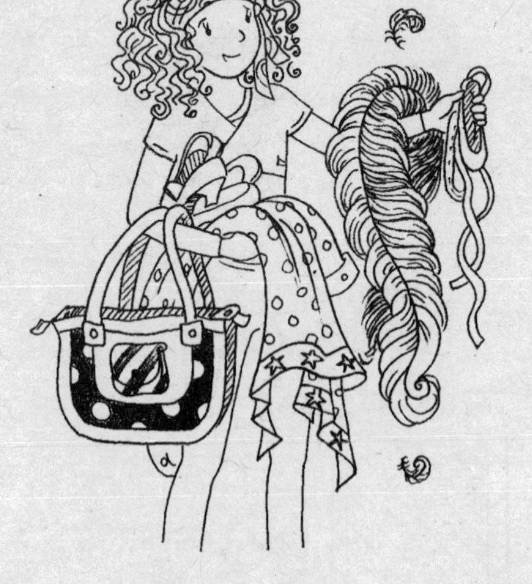

costumes and pairs of shoes, plus Sasha's bag, there was a lot to carry.

"Can we help?" Rachel offered.

"If we carry your things, Tamara could help you walk, Sasha," Kirsty suggested politely.

"Thank you, girls," Sasha said. "That would be really nice. I'll have to rest my foot and just hope it gets better quickly. The show must go on!"

The four of them went back to the star's trailer, which was painted bright turquoise and decorated with pink and purple butterflies. Once inside, Sasha sank gratefully into an armchair, while Tamara hung up the costumes. "We'll get you a drink," Rachel suggested, spotting the little kitchen through a doorway.

Sasha smiled. "Thank you," she said. "You're both so sweet, looking after me like this."

In the kitchen,

Kirsty found a glass and filled it with cold water. Meanwhile, Vanessa fluttered out of Rachel's pocket and waved her wand. "This will help Sasha's ankle," she said, as an ice pack magically appeared in Rachel's hand.

"Good idea," Rachel whispered as Vanessa darted back to her hiding place. "Thank goodness for fairy magic!"

She and Kirsty took the drink and ice pack to Sasha, who thanked them again. "That feels good," she sighed as Tamara put the ice pack on her swollen ankle.

"The sooner I can start practicing again, the better. I don't know what was wrong with me earlier. I can't understand it. If I dance that badly tonight, my fans will be really disappointed."

"You'll be fine," Tamara assured her, but Sasha didn't look so sure.

"I hope you feel better soon," Kirsty said. "We'd better go and practice the routine now. We'll see you later."

Once they were outside the trailer, Vanessa fluttered out of Rachel's pocket and the three friends exchanged worried looks. "I'm not feeling very hopeful about tonight." Rachel sighed. "We don't have much time before Sasha's show, and there's still no sign of your clef, Vanessa."

"Those boys were good in the dance class, weren't they?" Kirsty remembered. "You don't think . . ."

The thought occurred to them all at the same time. "They were goblins!" they cried together.

"They were dancing so well, one of them must be wearing my magic clef necklace," Vanessa realized. "There's no time to lose — we have to find those goblins!"

Kirsty Has a Plan!

Vanessa waved her wand at the girls, and a stream of sparkly stars swirled from its tip. In the next moment, Kirsty and Rachel had shrunk down to the size of fairies — and had their very own shimmering wings. "Let's fly!" Vanessa said, grinning at their delighted faces. She zoomed into the air, and Kirsty and Rachel followed.

The girls loved the feeling of soaring high above the festival crowds.

They flew around Star Village, where they'd last seen the goblins, hoping to spot them again. Although there were lots of people in the different tents, the three fairy friends didn't see any sign of the goblins at all.

"Maybe they're practicing their dance routines backstage," Rachel suggested. "Let's look there."

Despite searching all around the main stage and the backstage area, there was no sign of the goblins there, either. In fact, they still hadn't found them even after flying around the stars' trailers, the rehearsal tents, and all over the campsite.

"We searched everywhere. Where could they be?" Kirsty said, frowning.

Just then, they heard a faint musical beat. "Someone's listening to 'Let's Dance,'" Rachel said, recognizing the tune.

"And the music's coming from Rainspell Beach," Vanessa realized. "Let's look there!"

It was breezy down on the beach, and the three fairies had to battle against the wind to fly. But it was worth the struggle. Within minutes, they'd tracked the sound of the music to where they saw the goblins practicing their dance moves at the far end of the beach. They'd brought along an MP3 player with speakers, and were all dancing perfectly in time with the music.

"Let's hide behind these rocks and watch," Kirsty suggested, ducking down out of sight. Rachel and Vanessa followed. Then they all peeked out to watch the dancers.

The goblins were taking turns dancing solos, with athletic jumps and spins thrown in. "Woo-hoo!" one goblin cheered at the end of his routine. "Dancing is much more fun than being bossed around by Jack Frost."

"My turn!" another goblin announced impatiently. He grabbed something from the first goblin, and Rachel gasped as she caught a glimpse of it — Vanessa's magic clef!

"Did you see that?" she whispered excitedly to Kirsty and Vanessa. "The clef!"

"Yes," Vanessa said with a smile. "Let's try to think of a way to get it back."

Now the goblins were all fighting over the clef — pushing one another and grabbing at the necklace. "They're so busy fighting, they might not notice if a couple more goblins join in," Kirsty said thoughtfully. "Vanessa, do you think you could use your magic to turn me and Rachel into goblins?"

"Of course!" Vanessa said, waving her wand. A flood of fairy dust sparkled around Kirsty and Rachel, and the next moment they found their noses growing bigger . . . and greener!

Now Rachel and Kirsty looked just like goblins, complete with the same leotards as the four goblin dancers, who were still wrestling and arguing.

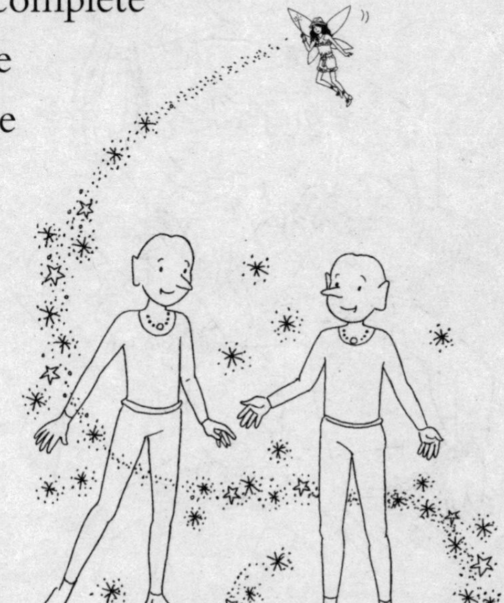

"You'll have to be quick," Vanessa warned.

"My magic isn't at full strength without my clef. The disguises won't last long."

"Then there's no time to lose," said Kirsty, her heart thumping. "Let's go!"

Rachel and Kirsty hurried over to the fighting goblins and joined in the noisy scuffle, hoping to grab the clef. The goblins were pushing and shoving as fiercely as ever, and Kirsty barely avoided being elbowed in the face. The sooner they could grab the clef the better, Rachel thought as she was jostled by a bossy goblin.

Then Kirsty noticed that the clef had fallen onto the sand. She dove down to get it.

Kirsty was just fighting her way back out of the crowd of goblins when a tall, skinny goblin saw her holding the clef and promptly tripped her.

The clef went flying out of Kirsty's hand — but, by a stroke of luck, Rachel made an amazing catch. Now *she* had it!

But not for long! A heavyset goblin with an enormous wart on his nose grabbed it right from her hand. As Rachel saw the clef vanish from her grasp, she saw something else starting to vanish, too . . . her goblin disguise! It was clear that Vanessa's magic was already wearing off. She and Kirsty had to get back to their hiding place before the goblins realized who they really were!

Dance-off Drama

Rachel nudged Kirsty and pointed out what was happening. Then both girls ran for the safety of the rocks, just in time. Once they were hidden out of sight, the last tinges of green faded from their skin and they were normal girls again.

"Oh, no," Kirsty whispered. "That didn't work as well as I had hoped."

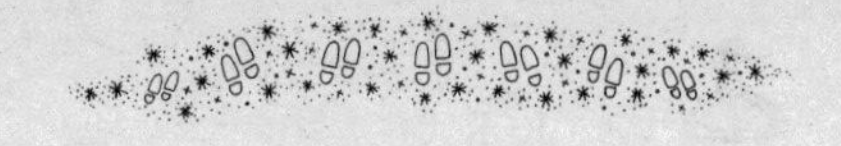

"It's getting close to six," Vanessa said. The fairy peeked at the watch as she fluttered to land on Rachel's wrist. "The goblins will be going back to the dance tent soon to find Tamara and Sasha for the rehearsal. We have to think of something quickly."

Vanessa's comment about the rehearsal gave Rachel an idea. "Vanessa, do you think you could use your magic to make one of us look like Tamara this time?" she asked.

She quickly explained her plan to her friends, and both Kirsty and Vanessa

smiled. "I love it!" Kirsty said. "Good thinking. Should I be Tamara?"

Vanessa looked anxiously at her wand. "I don't have a lot of magic left," she said. "Disguising Kirsty as Tamara and changing you back to fairy-size, Rachel, is going to use up the last of my power — so we have got to get this right. Otherwise . . ."

She didn't finish her sentence, but she didn't need to. Both Rachel and Kirsty knew that this was their last chance.

"We'll give it our best shot," Rachel promised.

Vanessa waved her wand and more of her sparkly magic poured out. There was just enough to turn Rachel back into a fairy, and to make Kirsty look like Tamara, with curly hair and a purple leotard. The magic also gave her a shiny gold cup to hold.

"In you go," Kirsty laughed, holding out the cup, and Vanessa and Rachel both flew inside.

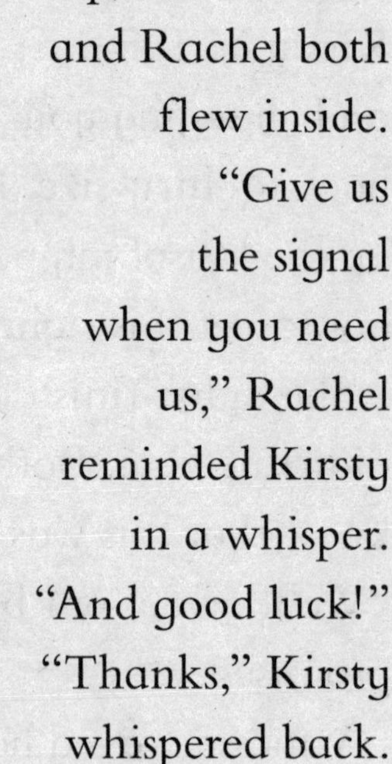

"Give us the signal when you need us," Rachel reminded Kirsty in a whisper. "And good luck!"

"Thanks," Kirsty whispered back.

"Here goes." She walked out from behind the rocks, straight up to the fighting goblins.

"Hi, boys," she said to them. "Remember me? I'm Tamara, Sasha Sharp's assistant."

The goblins immediately stopped fighting and stared in surprise.

"We're looking for new talent, and we both thought you danced amazingly well in class today," Kirsty went on. "In fact, Sasha thought one of you should get an award for such awesome dancing. The question is, who deserves it the most?"

There was a moment of stunned silence as the goblins took in this exciting news. Then they all shouted at once. "Me! I'm the best!"

"I should get the cup!"

"I can do a triple spin — on my head!"

"Whoa, whoa!" Kirsty said to the noisy goblins. "There's only one way to decide this. We'll have a dance-off — and I'll award the winner with this trophy. Who's going first?"

Peeking over the edge of the cup, Rachel noticed that one goblin had the magic clef necklace wrapped around his wrist. He was smirking. "I am so going to win this," he said to the others. "You might as well let me have the cup now!"

"That's not fair! You can't wear the clef for the dance-off," the warty-nosed goblin grumbled.

"Yeah, take it off," a third goblin insisted. "Or else you're not allowed to compete."

"All right, all right," grumbled the goblin with the clef. He took it off his wrist and made a big deal of leaving it on the sand. But then, while the other goblins weren't looking, he quickly tucked the clef into his sequined belt.

"Are we ready? Let's see the first dancer," Kirsty said, and pressed a button on the MP3 player to start the music.

The tallest goblin began to dance while the others watched. "He's not *awful*," Rachel whispered to Vanessa as they both peeked out. "But he definitely danced better when he had the clef."

Vanessa nodded. "His dancing is still pretty good because he's close to the clef," she explained in a whisper. "The closer they are to it, the better they'll be."

Then came the second dancer, who also danced well . . . until one of the other goblins slyly stuck out his foot and tripped him! He fell in a pile on the sand, looking furious. "That's cheating," he whined, and refused to try again.

Next was the dancer who'd secretly tucked the clef in his belt. He was *amazing.* He twirled and spun, hopped and jumped, and performed a string of complicated moves with a big smile on his face. Clearly, he was having a lot of fun showing off for an audience!

As he danced, the clef slid out from where he'd hidden it, and dangled temptingly from his belt. Rachel exchanged a glance with Vanessa. "Should we?" she whispered.

"Yes!" Vanessa whispered in reply.

Stage Magic

The two fairies snuck out of the golden cup and rushed toward the dancing goblin. They tried to get close enough to grab the clef without being noticed. It wasn't easy — the goblin was spinning himself around so quickly that Rachel started to feel dizzy from racing around after him.

Around and around she and Vanessa flew, and Rachel was just beginning to feel as if she'd never get close to the clef when the song ended, and the goblin struck a dramatic pose. Quick as lightning, Rachel zipped toward the clef and pulled it from the goblin's belt. She passed it to Vanessa and, with a bright flash of sparkles, the clef shrank down to its usual fairy size. Hooray — they'd done it!

The two fairies flew a safe distance from the goblin, smiling with delight.

The goblin, meanwhile, hadn't realized that the clef was gone and began dancing to the next tune. Of course, without the clef, he wasn't nearly as skillful, and he tripped over his big green feet within seconds.

Just then, Kirsty's disguise as Tamara began to wear off! The goblins stared as they realized what had happened. "We were tricked!" the tall one groaned, his head in his hands.

"Sorry," Kirsty said cheerfully as she helped up the goblin who'd fallen over.

"But you shouldn't take things that don't belong to you — and you definitely shouldn't try to cheat by using magic!"

As the goblins launched into a furious argument about whose fault it was that they didn't have the clef anymore, Kirsty skipped off to find Vanessa and Rachel, with a big smile on her face. They'd found the clef — now everyone's dance steps would fall into place!

Later that night, Kirsty and Rachel filed onto the stage with the other kids from the dance class. When they'd met for the rehearsal at six o'clock, Vanessa had used her dance magic to ensure that everyone danced wonderfully to Sasha's routine, including Sasha! They were all so good that it had been impossible for Sasha and Tamara to choose just a few dancers to

perform onstage. In the end, she picked them all, so the stage was very full.

"It's too bad those boys didn't come back," Kirsty heard Sasha saying to Tamara. "They were fabulous."

Kirsty grinned at Rachel. They could guess why the "boys" hadn't come back — they were probably in big trouble with Jack Frost for losing Vanessa's magic dance clef!

The lights dimmed onstage, and everyone stood in their starting positions. Then, as the opening notes of "Let's Dance" played, a roar of applause came from the audience and gave Rachel goose bumps. She couldn't believe she was here onstage at the Rainspell Island Music Festival, about to dance with Kirsty in front of thousands of people!

"I'd be nervous if it wasn't for you, Vanessa," Kirsty whispered. "I'm glad you're here with us!"

Vanessa, who was tucked inside Kirsty's pocket, grinned. "I wouldn't miss it for anything," she said.

"And now that I have my clef back, my choreography magic will make sure everyone dances like a dream!"

As Sasha launched into the first verse, the girls stopped talking and danced along with everyone else. When Rachel caught a glimpse of her parents clapping and waving in the audience, she felt like she might burst with happiness and pride.

"This has been the best day EVER," Kirsty said when the song finally came to an end and the audience cheered.

"I know," Rachel agreed, grinning. "Three fairy adventures in one day — that's a new record, Kirsty! And with four clefs left to find, who knows what will happen tomorrow?"

Kirsty smiled. "I can't wait to find out," she said happily.

THE SUPERSTAR FAIRIES

Vanessa has her magic clef back.
Now Kirsty and Rachel need to help

Miley
the Stylist Fairy!

Join their next adventure
in this special sneak peek. . . .

Clashing Clothes

"What's that noise?" Rachel murmured sleepily. She could hear a steady *pitter-patter* sound on the roof of the tent above her. Yawning, Rachel sat up in her sleeping bag. At the same time, her best friend, Kirsty, stirred and opened her eyes.

"Oh, it's *raining*!" Rachel exclaimed, suddenly realizing what the noise was.

Kirsty sat up, too. "Is that thunder?" she asked a little nervously as a loud rumble echoed through the tent.

Rachel laughed. "No, that's my dad snoring in the other section of the tent!" she explained. Scrambling out of her sleeping bag, she went over to the tent's main entrance. Kirsty followed, and together the two girls looked out.

The site of the Rainspell Island Music Festival was soggy with heavy rain. It was morning, but the sky was dark and threatening. The grassy fields where the tents, stages, and performers' trailers had been set up were already turning to mud.

"What a shame!" Kirsty remarked. "Especially when we had such amazing weather yesterday."

"It doesn't matter if it's sunny or rainy,

though, does it?" Rachel reminded her. "We still have to keep looking for the Superstar Fairies' magic clefs!"

Kirsty nodded. "I wonder which fairy we'll help today," she said.

"We saw three fantastic concerts yesterday, didn't we?" Rachel remarked as she and Kirsty went back to their sleeping area. "It's good that Jessie, Adele, and Vanessa got their clefs back in time, and that they had *just* enough magic to help The Angels, A-OK, and Sasha Sharp perform well."

"But the Superstar Fairies need *all* the magic clefs for things to be right again." Kirsty sighed. "And even though we've seen the goblins, we still haven't found Jack Frost! I wish we knew where he was hiding. . . ."

RAINBOW magic

These activities are magical!

Play dress-up, send friendship notes, and much more!

SCHOLASTIC

www.scholastic.com

www.rainbowmagiconline.com

RMACTIV3